By Cindy Dulaney

Chloe's Christmas Story

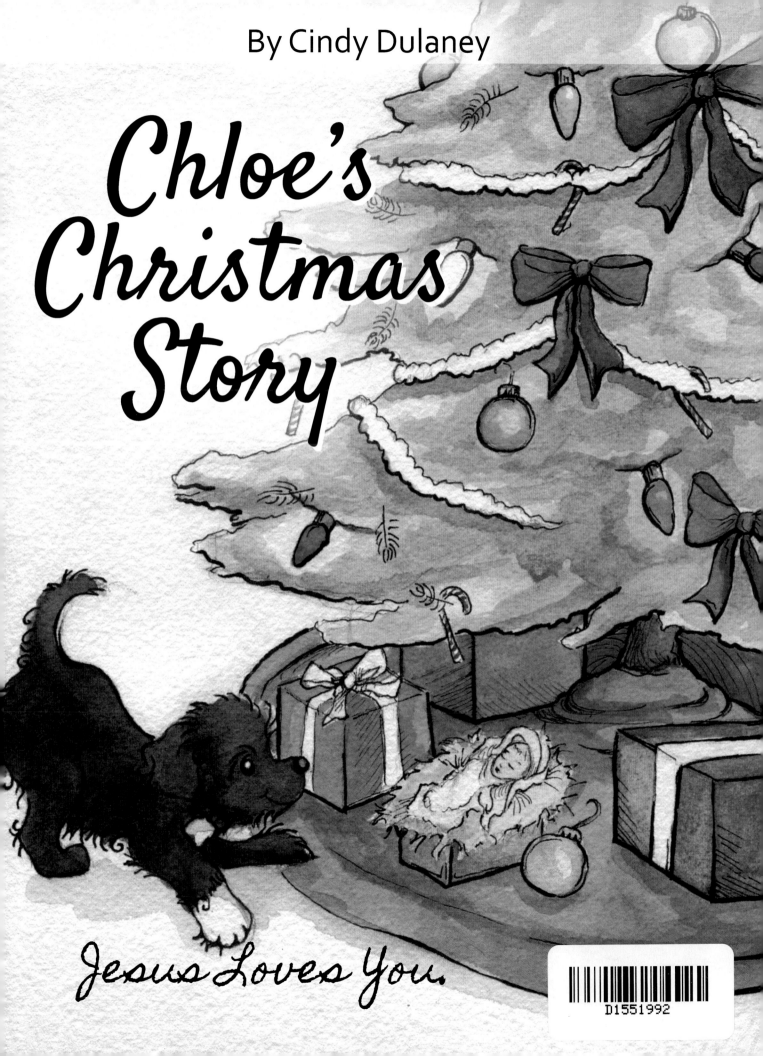

Jesus Loves You.

Dedication:

This Book is dedicated to Jesus for His great love for all of us.

I also dedicate this book to Chloe who was a very special dog that I was blessed to share 12 years with. She was my constant companion and so sweet. Chloe loved her family very much.
Chloe 2007 - 2020

Author: Cindy Dulaney

I grew up in Southeastern PA and loved all animals, especially dogs, all my life. My love for dogs started as a little girl when I had a poodle named GiGi. I also shared life with several other companion animals including: Favre, Baron, Dezi, Charlee, Gracie, and Ruthie.

Illustrator: Kelsey Showalter

I found Kelsey after searching for over a year for a great illustrator. Thank you Kelsey; I love your work and especially your images of Chloe.

Special thanks to my daughter-in-law Allison Dulaney. Her input was instrumental in helping me with this book.

A portion of the proceeds for the sale of this book will go to Christian organizations that support teaching children about the Love of GOD in Christ Jesus. I will also support organizations that continue nurturing children throughout their childhood into teenage and adult years. I believe it is a great calling to help children know how much God loves them.

A Note from the Author...

This book was inspired by God. All glory, honor, and praise belong to Him alone.

My hope for this book is that families will come together to learn about the love of God and the true meaning of Christmas.

My prayer is for all children and people to come to know the love and saving grace of Jesus Christ.

"But Jesus said, "Let the little children come to Me, and do not hinder them! For the kingdom of heaven belongs to such as these."
Matthew 19:14

"Hi, my name is Chloe.
I'm a Pomapoo,

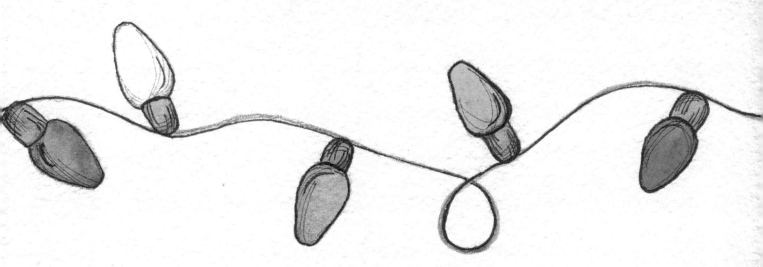

and I have good news for you!"

2

Christmas is such a magical time...

4

Snowmen, lights, trees, and gifts...

but what really was God's grand design?

There was a manger so long ago

that held a baby that you can know.

His name is Jesus.

He loves you and me.

That's the best present of all, you will see!

12

The gifts we give are like the gifts of God's Love,

that He sends from heaven above.

Even though Jesus is the Son of God,

He came as a little baby, isn't that odd?

"Why did He come?" you might say.

He came so that you can go to heaven one day!

Sin is when we do something wrong,

but Jesus forgives us and makes us strong.

As the Son of God, Jesus had no sin.

When we put our trust in HIM ------------- WE WIN !

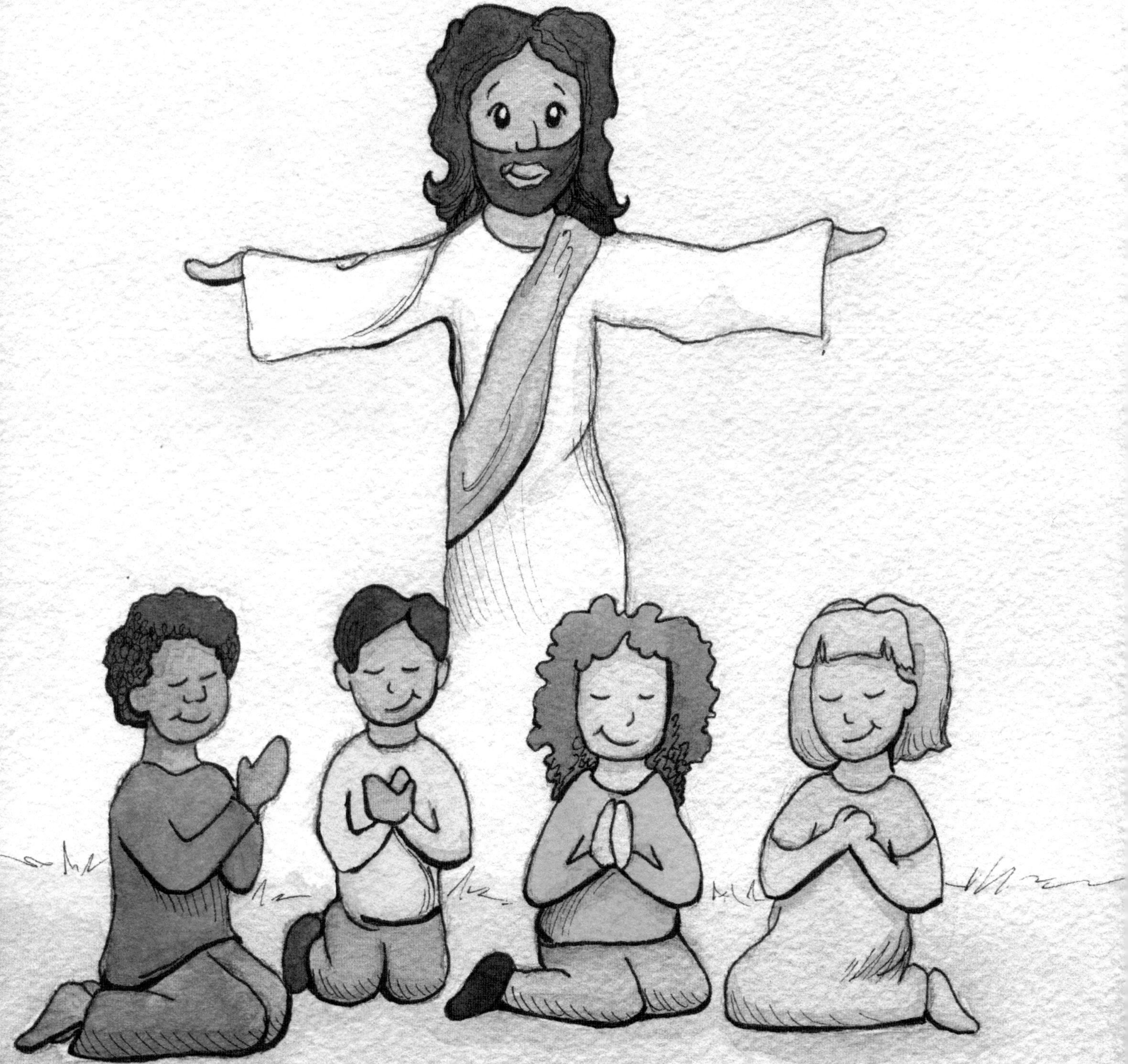

Because of His love Jesus wants us to love one another…

24

Mommy, Daddy, Sister, and Brother!

Take some time to show you care.

This can happen everywhere!

We are all God's creation.

Merry Christmas to all the nations!

Made in the USA
Monee, IL
10 December 2020